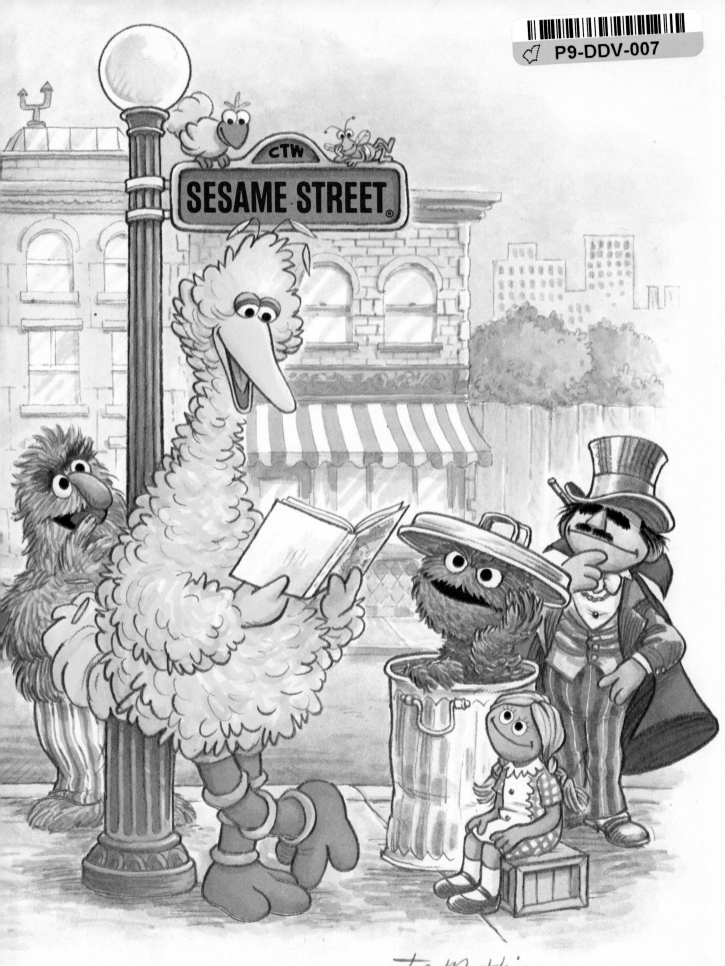

Joe Mathieu

THE SESAME STREET LIBRARY

With Jim Henson's Muppets

VOLUME 3

FEATURING
THE LETTERS
E AND F
AND THE NUMBER
3

Children's Television Workshop/Funk & Wagnalls, Inc.

WRITTEN BY:

Michael Frith
Emily Perl Kingsley
David Korr
Sharon Lerner
Nina B. Link
Jeffrey Moss
Norman Stiles
Daniel Wilcox

ILLUSTRATED BY:

Peter Cross
Michael Frith
Joseph Mathieu
Jon McIntosh
Harry McNaught
Marc Nadel
Kelly Oechsli
Michael J. Smollin
Caroll Spinney

PHOTOGRAPHS BY:

Charles P. Rowan

The Monster's Three Wishes

Once there lived a little monster
In a kingdom far away.
And a very strange thing happened
As he brushed his teeth one day.

As he squeezed his tube of toothpaste,
Deepest thunder shook the skies.
And suddenly a genie stood
Before his very eyes.

"I'm the genie of the toothpaste,"
Said the genie with a laugh.
"I've been trapped inside
                that toothpaste tube
For **3** weeks and a half.
You squeezed the tube and set me free
So here is what I'll do—
I'll let you have **3** wishes
And I'll make them all come true."

"Oh boy!" exclaimed the monster,
"Wow! **3** wishes just for me!
Now let me think and then decide
What my first wish will be."

Now my favorite thing is cookies,
Thought the monster with a grin.
*But first I'll wish for something nice
To keep my cookies in. .
I would like a million cookies,
But before I use that wish…*

"Hey, Genie," said the monster,
"Will you please bring me a <u>dish</u>?"

"Will I ever!" said the genie,
"For your wish is my command."
And instantly a dish appeared
Right in the monster's hand.

"Hey, I did it!" cried the genie.
"Wow! I haven't lost my touch!"
"It's a nice dish," said the monster,
"But it won't hold very much."

The monster thought of all the cookies
That he'd soon get with his wish.
And he knew a million cookies
Couldn't fit on one small dish.

He would need something much bigger.
So the monster said, "Hey, Genie!
I would like a great big box...
This plate is much too teeny!"

"You want a box? You've got it,"
Said the genie with a smirk.
And instantly a box appeared.
The monster cried, "Nice work!"

But although the box was pretty big
And could hold lots of stuff—
Could it hold a million cookies...?
It just wasn't big enough.

So the monster called the genie
And said, "Boy, am I in luck!
Since you'll give me what I wish for...
How about a great big <u>truck</u>?"

And right away a truck appeared
Before the monster's eyes.
"Fantastic!" cried the monster.
"It is just the perfect size!"

"It will hold a million cookies,
And I'll never have to worry.
And that is what I wish for!
Give me cookies now! Please hurry!"

"I am sorry," said the genie,
"For though cookies are delicious,
I *cannot* give them to you
'Cause you've used up your **3** wishes."

"Oh, no!" exclaimed the monster.
"Is it true? I just can't tell.
For although I'm good at eating things,
I do not count so well."

"Let us count these things together,"
Said the genie, "and you'll see—
The <u>dish</u> is **1**, the <u>box</u> is **2**,
And then the <u>truck</u> makes **3**."
"**3** things! You're right," the monster said,
"Now what am I to do?
I've used up my **3** wishes
And I'm very hungry, too!"

"Gee, that's too bad," the genie said,
"But now my job's complete."
"I'm so *hungry*," said the monster,
"Oh, I need something to *eat!*"

"I'm sad your wish for cookies
Can't come true," the genie said.
"That's okay," replied the monster........

"...I'll just eat the <u>truck</u> instead!"

And as the monster ate the truck,
The genie disappeared,
Saying, "I have seen a lot of things—
But boy...is *that* guy weird!"

Big Bird Visits His Cousin

Here is a picture of me coming to visit
my cousin Bunscombe, the baker.

This is cousin Bunscombe Bird. He
is carrying a delicious birdseed pie.

Another cousin has arrived. Oh goody! It is police
officer Bertha Bird. She is one of my favorites!

Now Fire Chief Bagshot
Bird is here, too.

The last one to come is my cousin
Bathsheba Bird, the doctor.

And here we all are. Isn't it nice that
so many cousins came to call today?

Hey, Mr. Hooper, do you have any extra paper bags? Maria and I want to show the kids how to make Front and Back Masks.

Why, yes, David. Here they are. But tell me, what's a Front and Back Mask?

O.K., Mr. Hooper. But first, do you have a pair of scissors we could use?

Here they are, David. Now—what is a Front and Back Mask?

Just a minute, Mr. Hooper. Do you have some crayons we can borrow?

Sure, sure, sure, Maria. NOW will you tell me what a Front and Back Mask is?

Just as soon as you give us some yarn and sticky tape, Mr. Hooper.

O.K.! O.K.! Here they are. NOW . . . will you PLEASE tell me . . . WHAT *IS* A FRONT AND BACK MASK?

Here it is, Mr. Hooper! Now no one will know who you are.

Oh, hi, Mr. Blooper. Gee, you're looking very well today. Did you get a haircut or something?

SPINNEY

HOW TO MAKE A FRONT AND BACK MASK

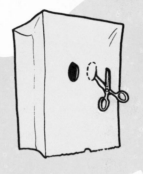

1. Find a paper bag big enough to fit over your head.

2. Cut two holes in the bag for eyes.

If you want to, you can cut holes for your nose and mouth, too.

3. Draw a funny face on the front of the mask.

FRONT   BACK

FRONT   BACK

STICK YARN ON WITH GLUE OR STICKY-TAPE!

4. Stick yarn or string on the bag for hair.

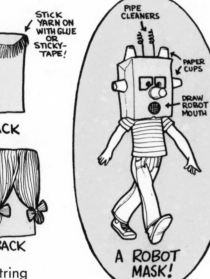

PIPE CLEANERS

PAPER CUPS

DRAW ROBOT MOUTH

A ROBOT MASK!

YOU ARE SO CUTE!

If you really want to surprise people, draw a face on the front, and *another* face on the back. Your friends won't know if you're coming or going.

Oh, yeah? Well, with the mask I'm making . . .

. . . people will know if *I'm* coming or going . . .

. . . I'm *ALWAYS* going!

The Emperor's New Clothes

Once there was an emperor who loved new clothes. He owned 6,372 suits already, but still he wanted more.

One day two crafty thieves came to the palace.

"We can make you a suit of gold and silver and pearls the like of which you have never seen," they told the emperor.

The foolish emperor gave them the silver and gold, and heaps of pearls, and told them to make the fabulous suit.

"It will be a magic suit," said the thieves. "Only people who are very, *very* wise—people like yourself, dear emperor—will be able to see it."

As soon as the emperor had left, the thieves quickly hid the silver and gold and pearls in their knapsack. Then they pretended to cut and sew. But, actually, they were cutting and sewing nothing but thin air.

At last the thieves said the suit was ready. They held up their empty hands. "Isn't it beautiful?" they cried.

"Superb," said the emperor, because he did not want anyone to think he was not wise.

"Superb," said everyone in the palace, for they did not want the emperor to think *they* were not wise.

The emperor paraded through town to show off his new clothes.

Suddenly a little boy shouted, "Why, look! The emperor isn't wearing any clothes at all!"

"The child is right!" shouted everyone.

And the silly emperor ran back to his palace as fast as he could go.

Ernie Plants a Garden

Cookie Monster, Baker

The Count, Cashier

The Perils of Penelope

(continued)

As you remember from Volume 2, Penelope was being carried away by a giant bird.

Unfortunately, the bird thought Penelope's head was an egg, so she took Penelope to her nest and sat on her.

Ernie, get me out from under this bird.

You think you've got problems? I can't find my goggles.

Just in the nick of time, a Young-Hero-Lumberjack cut the branch with his trusty ax and got Penelope down.

Unfortunately, Penelope landed right on the foot of a giant.

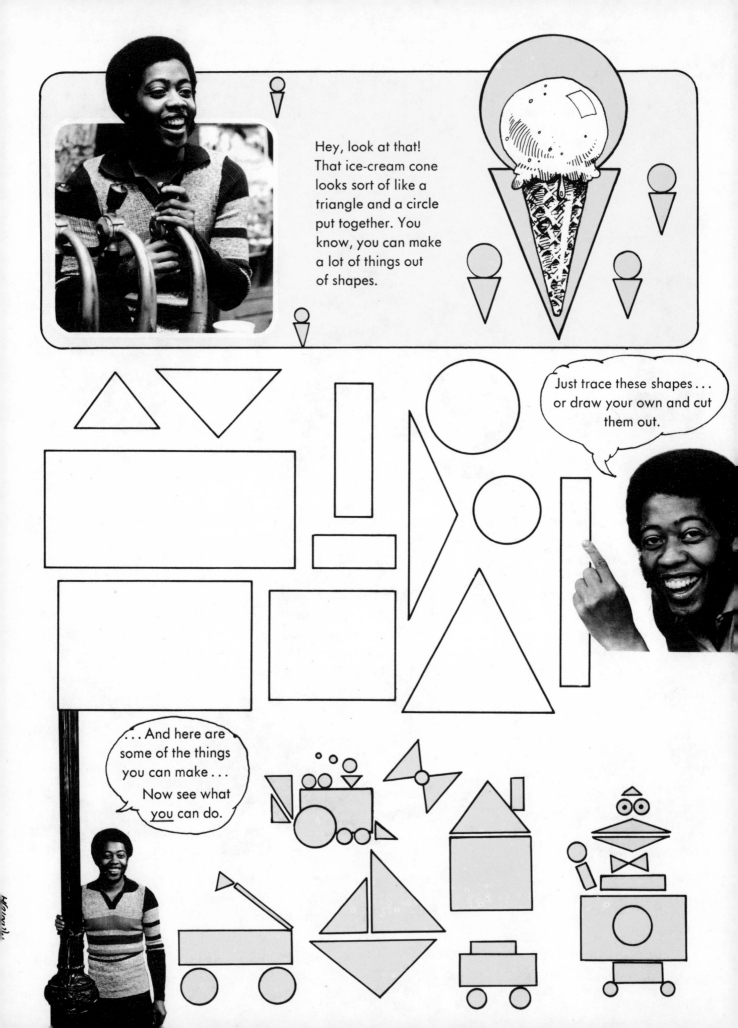

Hey, look at that! That ice-cream cone looks sort of like a triangle and a circle put together. You know, you can make a lot of things out of shapes.

Just trace these shapes... or draw your own and cut them out.

...And here are some of the things you can make... Now see what you can do.

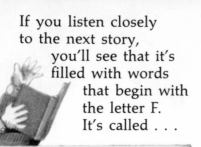 If you listen closely
to the next story,
    you'll see that it's
filled with words
    that begin with
    the letter F.
    It's called . . .

Once upon a time, there was a famous fireman named Fat Fireman
Foster. Fat Fireman Foster was famous because he was a fabulous
fire fighter and because all his names began with the letter F.

One Friday in February, Fat Fireman Foster was driving his fancy
fire truck through a forest when all of a sudden he saw some
smoke! "Where there's smoke, there's fire!" said Fat Fireman Foster.
"And since this is a forest, that must be a forest fire! Never fear,"
called Fat Fireman Foster. "Fat Fireman Foster is here!"

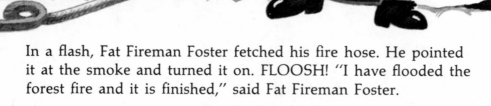

In a flash, Fat Fireman Foster fetched his fire hose. He pointed
it at the smoke and turned it on. FLOOSH! "I have flooded the
forest fire and it is finished," said Fat Fireman Foster.

But when the smoke cleared, Fat Fireman Foster found that it
had not been a forest fire at all!

"Oh, no!" said Fat Fireman Foster. "I figured it was a forest fire—
but it was a frankfurter fire instead! Just a few friendly folks
fixing frankfurters! Oh, I'm sorry, folks," said Fat Fireman Foster.
"Can you ever forgive me?"

"Sure, we'll forgive you!" said the folks. "We still have our frankfurters.
And we have our fins and flippers, too. Fortunately we know how to
swim and eat at the same time. Come join the fun, Fat Fireman Foster!"

So Fat Fireman Foster joined the fun and had a fabulous time
feeding on frankfurters and flipping the flippers he borrowed
from his new-found friends.

There are two things to be learned from the fable of Fat Fireman Foster:

Number one is:
Sometimes things are not
what you think they are.

Number two is:
The names Fat, Fireman,
and Foster all begin
with the letter F.